THE TINDER BOX

Retold by Michael Bedard   Illustrated by Regolo Ricci

TORONTO OXFORD NEW YORK
OXFORD UNIVERSITY PRESS
1990

Oxford University Press, 70 Wynford Drive, Don Mills, Ontario, M3C 1J9

Toronto   Oxford   New York   Delhi   Bombay   Calcutta   Madras   Karachi
Petaling Jaya   Singapore   Hong Kong   Tokyo   Nairobi   Dar es Salaam
Cape Town   Melbourne   Auckland

and associated companies in
Berlin   Ibadan

Design: Kathryn Cole

Text © Michael Bedard 1990
Illustrations © Regolo Ricci 1990

Oxford is a trademark of Oxford University Press
1 2 3 4 – 3 2 1 0
Printed in Hong Kong

Canadian Cataloguing in Publication Data
Bedard, Michael, 1949–
The tinder box

A retelling of the story by Hans Christian Andersen.
ISBN 0-19-540767-9

I. Ricci, Regolo. II. Andersen, H.C. (Hans Christian), 1805–1875. The tinder box.
III. Title.

PS8553.E336T56 1990   jC813'.54   C89-095087-3   PZ8.B433Ti 1990

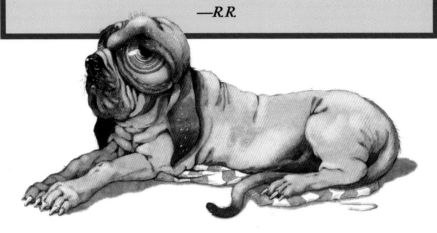

NE, TWO! ONE, TWO! The soldier came marching down the road, with his knapsack on his back and his sword swinging by his side. And though he'd not a penny to his name, he was happy, for he'd been off to the wars and was now on his way home.

As he walked along he happened upon an old woman standing at the side of the road.

"Good day," said she. "My, what a fine sword you have there, young man, and such a large knapsack. You're a brave soldier, I can see, and you shall have as much money as you wish."

"And how is that, good woman?" asked the soldier.

"Do you see that tree?" said the woman, pointing to a twisted old oak nearby. "It's hollow inside, and if you climb to the top you'll see a hole you can let yourself down through into the trunk."

"But what should I do in there?" asked the soldier.

"Fetch money, of course," said the woman with a smile. "I could tie a rope around your waist and lower you inside, and when you want out, you need but call and I'll haul you up again. Of course, though, if you're frightened ..."

"Frightened?" laughed the soldier. "Tie that rope around my waist, old woman, and I'll go down inside your tree."

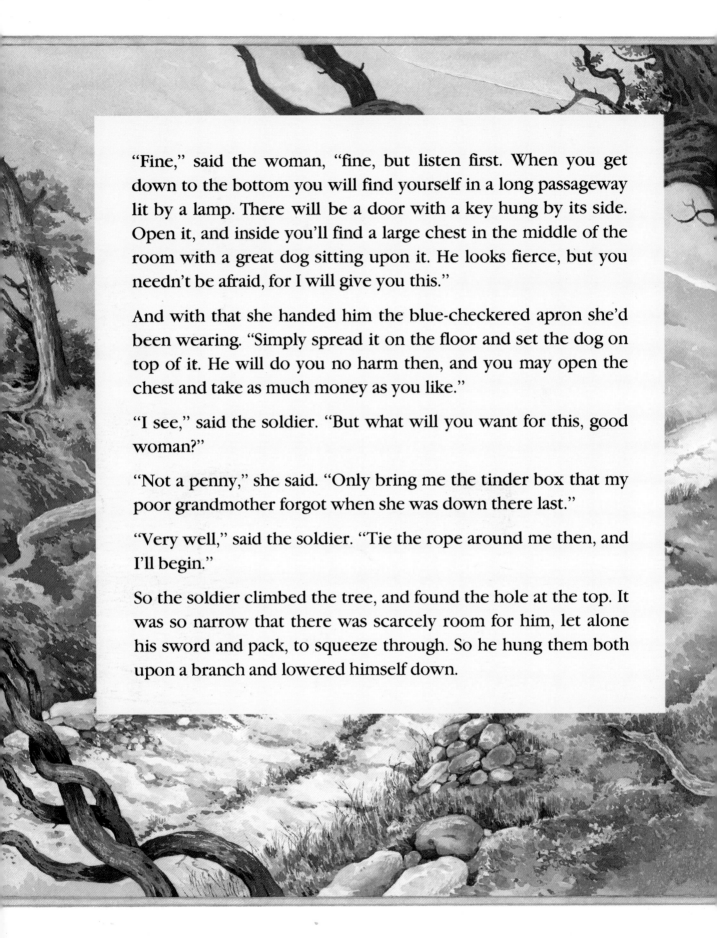

"Fine," said the woman, "fine, but listen first. When you get down to the bottom you will find yourself in a long passageway lit by a lamp. There will be a door with a key hung by its side. Open it, and inside you'll find a large chest in the middle of the room with a great dog sitting upon it. He looks fierce, but you needn't be afraid, for I will give you this."

And with that she handed him the blue-checkered apron she'd been wearing. "Simply spread it on the floor and set the dog on top of it. He will do you no harm then, and you may open the chest and take as much money as you like."

"I see," said the soldier. "But what will you want for this, good woman?"

"Not a penny," she said. "Only bring me the tinder box that my poor grandmother forgot when she was down there last."

"Very well," said the soldier. "Tie the rope around me then, and I'll begin."

So the soldier climbed the tree, and found the hole at the top. It was so narrow that there was scarcely room for him, let alone his sword and pack, to squeeze through. So he hung them both upon a branch and lowered himself down.

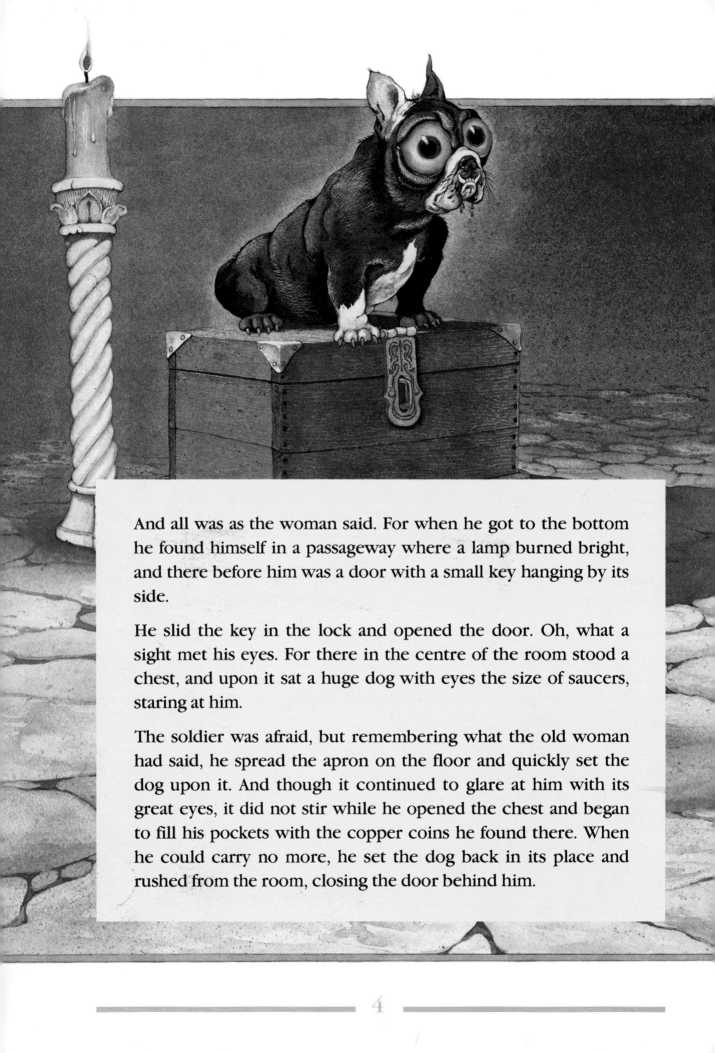

And all was as the woman said. For when he got to the bottom he found himself in a passageway where a lamp burned bright, and there before him was a door with a small key hanging by its side.

He slid the key in the lock and opened the door. Oh, what a sight met his eyes. For there in the centre of the room stood a chest, and upon it sat a huge dog with eyes the size of saucers, staring at him.

The soldier was afraid, but remembering what the old woman had said, he spread the apron on the floor and quickly set the dog upon it. And though it continued to glare at him with its great eyes, it did not stir while he opened the chest and began to fill his pockets with the copper coins he found there. When he could carry no more, he set the dog back in its place and rushed from the room, closing the door behind him.

He was ready to tug on the rope and have the woman haul him up, when suddenly he caught sight of a second door a little further along the passageway, and hanging on the wall beside it another, larger key. He lifted it down, slid it in the lock, and slowly eased open the door.

And what did he see within, but a larger chest and sitting upon it a still larger dog, this one with eyes the size of silver platters. When the dog caught sight of him, it began to growl. Oh, how the soldier wished he had his sword by his side and had not left it hanging useless on the tree. But his eyes lingered on the large trunk, and remembering the old woman's apron, he ran into the room, threw it down, and quickly set the beast upon it. And though it growled fiercely and glared at him with its great eyes, it did not stir from that place.

The soldier opened the lid of the chest. And there lay more silver than he had ever seen. Straight away he emptied his pockets of the pennies and filled them up with silver instead. And he filled his hat as well. Then he closed the chest, set the dog back on it, and ran from that room as fast as his legs could carry him.

But he had scarcely closed the door when still further down the hall he noticed a dim light creeping out from yet another door. He stole down there, and taking down the huge key from the wall beside it, he opened this door as well.

Immediately he wished he had not. For there, on a chest twice
as large as the last, sat a monstrous dog with eyes the size of
spinning wheels, whirling round and round in their sockets. The
dog leapt up, snapped its horrible jaws and howled. The poor
soldier's heart nearly stopped, and the hat full of silver fell to
the floor. He would have slammed the door shut then and there,
but his eyes fell on the chest the beast sat upon. And he took
courage and rushed into the room. Closing his eyes, he lifted
the creature down onto the apron. And though it filled the
room with its horrible howls, it would not stir from that place.

The soldier lifted the lid of the chest and gasped. For there lay more gold than he had ever dreamed of. He took one look and immediately began to imagine all the things he might do with it if it were his. Instantly he threw down all the silver he had gathered from the second room, and he began to stuff his pockets and his cap and even his poor boots to the brim with gold, so that he could hardly move when he was done. All the while the great dog glared at him and its eyes turned round and round in its head. Finally, he set the beast back on the chest and fled from that room and down the hall, tugging on the rope as he ran.

"Haul me up, old woman," he shouted up the tree.

"Have you got the tinder box?" asked the woman.

But no! He had quite forgotten it in his greed. So he went back to fetch it, and he found the old thing lying in the dust by the first door. Then the woman hauled him up, and a hard time she had of it, too, with all the gold he carried. But at last he found himself safely back beside her on the road.

"Ah," said the woman, eyeing the gold. "So, you found the other rooms, I see. A very brave young man, indeed. But now, where is my box?"

"What do you want it for, I wonder," said the soldier, turning the tarnished thing over in his hand.

"That's none of your affair," snapped the old woman. "You've got your money — and more. Now give me the box."

"Not until you tell me why you want it so," said the soldier. For since the woman had deceived him once about the doors, he thought there might be more here, too, than met the eye.

At this the old woman grew furious, and as her fury mounted, her face twisted horribly and her eyes burned in her head. Before his eyes, the nails on her fingers turned to talons and the teeth in her head to terrible fangs. And where the old woman had been, now stood a witch in her true shape.

"You will give it to me now," she spat, and sprang at him.

But in his terror the soldier drew his sword and with one desperate blow struck off the witch's head. Down it fell to the road with a dreadful shriek, and was still. The soldier scooped up all his scattered gold and fled that place, and not once did he dare look back.

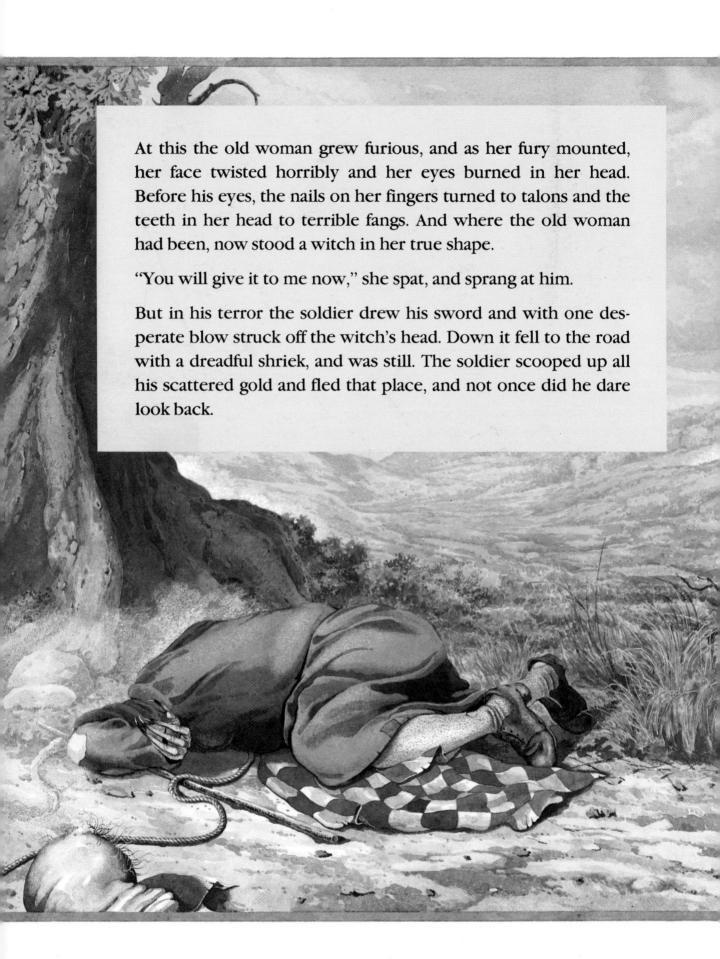

At last he came to a town, where he took a room in an inn. And when he had quite recovered from his fright, thoughts of the gold again filled his mind. So he ordered himself the finest food and drink, for now he was a wealthy man indeed, though the servant who cleaned his boots that night thought them rather shabby things for such a man as this.

The next day the soldier set out to buy himself some fine new clothes and the best boots money could buy. While they waited on him, the shopkeepers told the fine young gentleman about their town, and of their king and his beautiful daughter. A sad story it was, too, for it seemed the king kept the princess shut in a great copper castle all ringed round with towers and walls. No one had seen her in many a year, for it had been foretold that one day she would marry a common soldier, and the king would sooner shut her away forever than have such a thing come to pass.

"How I should like to see her," thought the soldier. But there seemed no way of doing so, even though now that he was rich he had many fine friends who flattered him and told him what a wonderful fellow he was. Yet while he often went to plays and rode in the royal park, he still gave much of his money to the poor, for he remembered all too well what it was like to be without a penny.

Now, since he was always spending money and never making more, he all too soon came to the end of it and had to leave behind the fine rooms he'd been living in. He rented an attic in a poorer part of town, and there he had to mend his clothes and clean his own boots. And none of his new friends came to see him, for there were too many stairs to climb.

One evening, as the dark was drawing near and he found he had not even enough money left to buy a candle, he recalled that in the tinder box he'd taken from the witch there was an old candle end. He went to fetch it, but no sooner had he struck a spark from the flint than the door flew open and in bounded the dog with eyes as big as saucers.

"What is my master's wish?" it said.

The soldier leapt up in astonishment. But the dog stood staring with its wide eyes, and said again:

"What is my master's wish?"

"Why, money, of course," said the soldier. And *whoosh*, away went the dog. And *whoosh*, it was back again before the soldier could blink an eye. But this time it had a bag of copper coins in its teeth.

And now the soldier understood the magic of the tinder box. For if he struck it once, the dog that watched the copper chest would appear, and if twice, the dog that watched the silver was there, and if three times, there stood the dog that guarded the chest of gold.

So the soldier moved back to his fine rooms again, and wore his fine clothes, and once again his friends came round, and were all, of course, as fond of him as ever they'd been before. But he knew them too well now, and his thoughts turned more and more to the princess shut in the copper castle, and he wished with all his heart that he might see her once.

So late one night he took up the tinder box as he sat alone, and struck it twice, and there stood the dog with eyes the size of platters.

"It is late, I know," he said. "But, if only for a moment, I should like to see the princess from the copper castle."

Away flew the dog and in an instant returned, with the princess lying fast asleep upon its back. She was so lovely to look upon that the soldier could not help but kiss her once before the dog whisked her away.

Come morning, the princess told the king and queen of the strange dream she'd had — of a dog that carried her on its back, and a soldier who had kissed her.

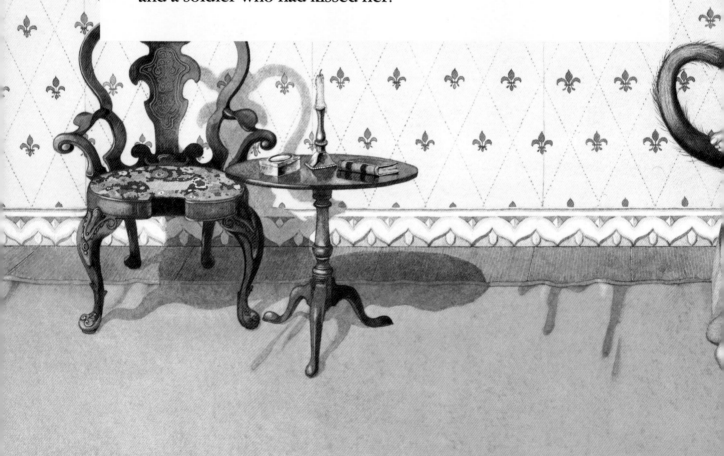

"A fine tale, indeed," cried the king.

And that night he set one of the ladies-in-waiting to watch by the princess's bed to see what she might see. And in the night the dog with eyes the size of platters came and carried the girl off on its back. But the woman ran after them and made a mark in chalk on the door of the house they went into so that she might know the place. Then she stole back to the palace, and by and by the dog came back with the princess as well.

But when the dog saw the mark on the soldier's house, it went and made the same mark on all the doors in town. So that when the king and queen and all the rest came the next day, they could not tell one house from another.

Then the queen, who was a clever woman, took her golden scissors and cut a bit of silk and made a bag. And she filled it with flour and tied it on the princess's back, and snipped a piece from the corner of it, so that the flour would trickle out behind the princess wherever she went.

That night the dog with eyes the size of spinning wheels came and carried the sleeping princess off to the soldier once more. And now he was so much in love with her that he wished with all his heart to marry her.

But the dog did not notice the little trail of flour that trickled from the bag all the way from the castle to the window of the soldier's room.

In the morning the king and queen well knew where their daughter had been, and the poor soldier was shut into prison and told that he would die the next day.

What a dark and dismal place it was, with nothing but a patch of shuttered light on the floor from the narrow window set in the wall above him. And through that window all night long came the dreadful thud of hammers as the gallows went up where he would be hanged. And now without the tinder box he had not a hope left in his heart.

Morning came at last, and with it the din of drums and soldiers marching, and the eager crowd hurrying from their houses to see the hanging. Among them was a shoemaker's boy, who ran at such a rate that one of his shoes flew off and landed by the prison window where the soldier watched.

"Boy," he cried, "come here. There's no hurry. Nothing will happen without me, I assure you. If you will run to my rooms and bring me the tinder box you'll find there, there will be gold for you. But you must hurry."

Away ran the boy and soon enough was back again.

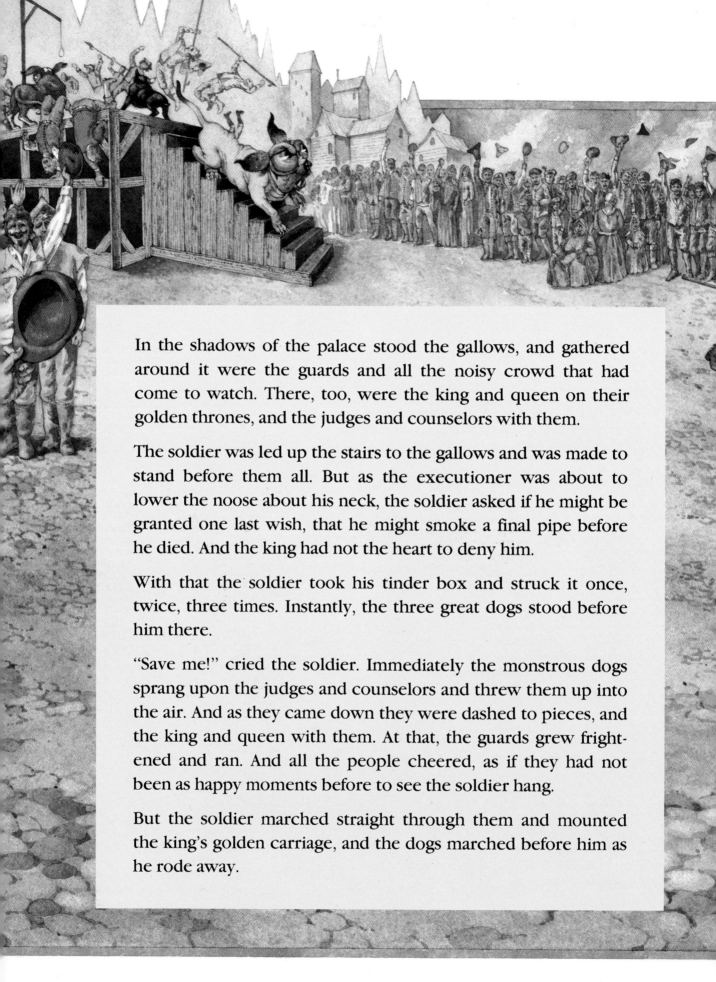

In the shadows of the palace stood the gallows, and gathered around it were the guards and all the noisy crowd that had come to watch. There, too, were the king and queen on their golden thrones, and the judges and counselors with them.

The soldier was led up the stairs to the gallows and was made to stand before them all. But as the executioner was about to lower the noose about his neck, the soldier asked if he might be granted one last wish, that he might smoke a final pipe before he died. And the king had not the heart to deny him.

With that the soldier took his tinder box and struck it once, twice, three times. Instantly, the three great dogs stood before him there.

"Save me!" cried the soldier. Immediately the monstrous dogs sprang upon the judges and counselors and threw them up into the air. And as they came down they were dashed to pieces, and the king and queen with them. At that, the guards grew frightened and ran. And all the people cheered, as if they had not been as happy moments before to see the soldier hang.

But the soldier marched straight through them and mounted the king's golden carriage, and the dogs marched before him as he rode away.

Straight away the soldier freed the princess from her copper prison, and by and by she became his wife. Their wedding feast lasted a week, they say, and the dogs sat at the table with them all the while, watching with their wondrous eyes.

THE END